Cabbage Patch Kids

Visit the Doctor

by M.J. Carr   Illustrated by Cathy Beylon

SCHOLASTIC INC.
New York Toronto London Auckland Sydney

ISBN 0-590-46631-3

Copyright © 1993 by Original Appalachian Artworks, Inc.
All rights reserved. Published by Scholastic Inc., by arrangement with Original
Appalachian Artworks, Inc., P.O. Box 714, Cleveland, GA 30528.
CABBAGE PATCH KIDS® is a registered trademark of Original Appalachian
Artworks, Inc.

12 11 10 9 8 7 6 5 4 3 2 1   3 4 5 6 7 8/9
Printed in the U.S.A.   24
First Scholastic printing, February 1993

Jessie had a cold. On Monday she had a
scratchy throat. On Wednesday she started snif-
fling and sneezing. And by Friday, Jessie was
coughing so hard she could barely sleep at night.

"Lora Lee has a cold, too," she told her dad.
"Her cold is much worse than mine."

Before Jessie went to bed, her mother rubbed a sticky gel on Jessie's chest. It felt warm and had a strong smell, like medicine.

"Lora Lee needs something for her cough, too," said Jessie. She blew on her fingers so they were warm, then rubbed them on Lora Lee's chest. She held Lora Lee tightly as she fell off to sleep. That way they could get better together.

But Jessie and Lora Lee didn't get much better. At least not that night. The room was still dark when Jessie woke up coughing. Her mother and father were in the room with her. They were talking in low voices, using words that Jessie didn't understand. She heard her mother say, "Maybe she has bronchitis." She heard her father say, "Then she'll need antibiotics." Jessie was coughing too hard to ask questions.

The next morning, when she woke up, she heard her mother on the phone talking to Dr. Cole.

"No, Mom!" said Jessie. "I can't go to the doctor! I have to stay in bed! You told me so!"

Her head was stuffed up and her chest felt heavy and sore. Jessie started to cry.

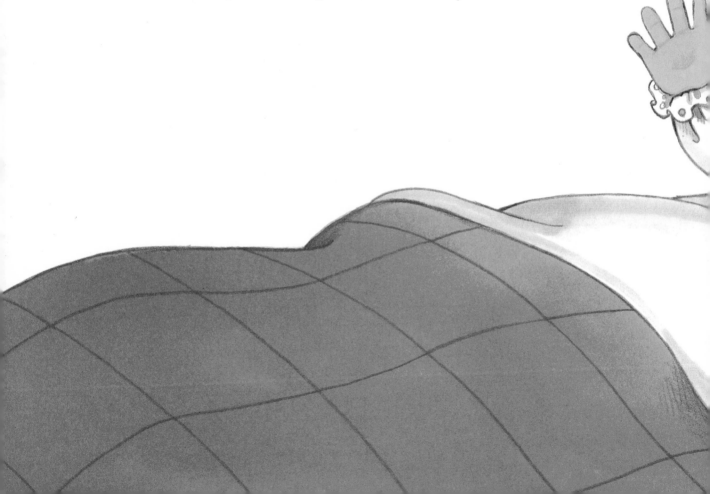

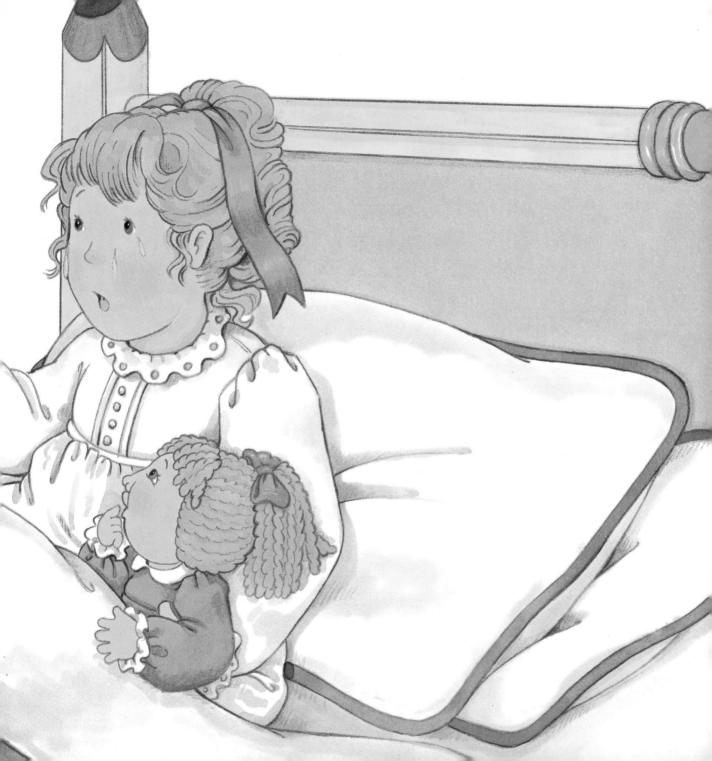

Jessie's mother wrapped her in her arms and kissed her hot forehead. Then she picked up Lora Lee. She felt Lora Lee's forehead. "It looks like Lora Lee is going to have to go to the doctor, too," she said. "I don't think she's ever been to see Dr. Cole before, has she?"

"No," said Jessie.

"Maybe you'd better tell her what it's like. That way she won't be so scared."

And so, while her mother dressed her warmly for the cold outdoors, Jessie told Lora Lee all about the doctor's office. She told Lora Lee that Dr. Cole might want to listen to her heart with a stethoscope. "Sometimes the stethoscope feels cold on your skin," she said. "But it never hurts."

She told Lora Lee that Dr. Cole would probably take her temperature with a thermometer. "She puts it under your tongue," she said. "It tastes a little funny, but not too bad. You have to be careful to keep your mouth closed until it's done."

Next she told Lora Lee about tongue depressors. "They're like Popsicle sticks," she explained. "Dr. Cole will tell you to open your mouth and say, 'Ah.' Then she'll press down on your tongue with the flat stick so she can see inside."

Lora Lee looked scared. "Don't worry," said Jessie. "That doesn't hurt at all."

"Ready to go?" asked Jessie's mom.
Jessie looked at Lora Lee. "I think so," she said. The three of them walked to the car.

In the car, Jessie tried to think of other things she should tell Lora Lee about the doctor's office. "Maybe Dr. Cole will put the ear scope in your ear," she said. "She puts it in just a little. Then she looks inside."

Then she remembered the X-ray machine.
"Dr. Cole puts a heavy blanket over you and takes
a picture. It shows what you look like inside. But
I don't think you'll need that," she said quickly.
"Not for a cold."

Jessie settled back in her seat and watched the trees streak by. She was starting to feel proud. Just last year, when she'd broken her arm, she'd had her picture taken by the X-ray machine. She hadn't realized how much she knew. Maybe someday she would be a doctor herself.

But Lora Lee still looked worried. She leaned in close to whisper to Jessie. "What about shots?" she asked.

"Oh, yeah. Shots," said Jessie. "Dr. Cole puts medicine inside a syringe. Then she gives you a shot and the medicine goes inside you to make you better."

"And that hurts, right?" asked Lora Lee.

Jessie didn't want to lie. "It does hurt, but just a little," she said. "It feels like a pinch for a second and then it's over."

"Here we are," said Jessie's mom. She pulled the car into the parking lot outside of Dr. Cole's office. When they entered the office they saw lots of other children in the waiting room.

"See," Jessie told Lora Lee. "Everyone comes to the doctor's."

Jessie, Jessie's mom, and Lora Lee sat in the waiting room, too. Jessie helped Lora Lee read books while they waited to go in to see the doctor. Jessie started to cough again. It made her feel tired to cough so hard. Jessie snuggled into her mom's lap.

"Dr. Cole's going to help you feel better," her mom said.

Finally, it was their turn. A nurse called their
name and brought them into the doctor's examin-
ing room. "It smells different than houses do,"
Jessie explained to Lora Lee. Then Jessie spotted
the scale. She'd forgotten to tell Lora Lee that the
doctor might put her on the scale to weigh her.
But it didn't matter because just then Dr. Cole
walked in.

Dr. Cole was a friendly doctor. She always said hello to Jessie and she always smiled. "So, I hear you have a cough," she said.

"Lora Lee, too," said Jessie.

"Well, let's take a look at you both."

Dr. Cole put a thermometer under Jessie's tongue. She put one in Lora Lee's mouth, too. Jessie wanted to remind Lora Lee not to be scared, but she knew she musn't talk with the thermometer in her mouth.

"Yes," said Dr. Cole when she took it out. "You do have a little bit of a temperature. A hundred and one." She showed Jessie the numbers on the thermometer so she could see, too.

"Now," said Dr. Cole. "Let's take a look at that throat of yours." She unwrapped a tongue depressor. Jessie went first so Lora Lee would see how easy it was.

Then Dr. Cole put the stethoscope on Jessie's chest and told her to breathe in and out and cough at the same time. "See," Jessie told Lora Lee when it was her turn. "I told you. It doesn't hurt at all."

While Dr. Cole sat down and talked with Jessie's mother, Jessie held Lora Lee close to her. Dr. Cole wrote out a prescription for some medicine Jessie would have to take at home. Then Jessie saw Dr. Cole reach for the syringe.

"Lora Lee first," said Jessie.

Dr. Cole nodded. She explained to Lora Lee that it would only hurt for a second, sort of like a little pinch.

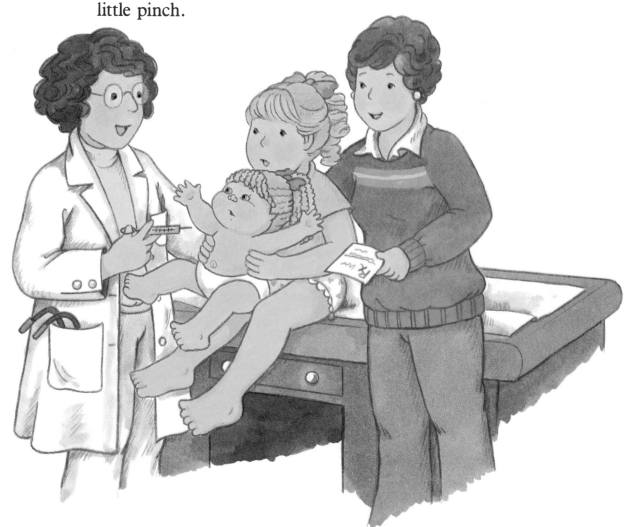

Then it was Jessie's turn. She closed her eyes, and Dr. Cole gave her the shot. Jessie hardly felt it at all.

"It's over?" she asked.

"Sure is," said Dr. Cole. She wiped Jessie's arm with a cotton ball and alcohol. "Two brave girls," she said. "I'm so glad to have a visit today from two such very brave girls."

Jessie smiled a big smile at Lora Lee.

On the ride home, they stopped at the pharmacy to pick up their medicine. Now Jessie was glad to get back home and under her covers with Lora Lee. Jessie's mom gave each of them a spoonful of the medicine. Then she brought them a big stack of books to read in bed.

"Once upon a time . . ." Jessie started to read to Lora Lee. But before she could turn the page, her eyes began to slip shut. Maybe Lora Lee needed a nap, she thought, to help her start to feel better. Jessie pulled the covers up around both of them and nestled down into her pillow. It had been a long, full day.